Story Tim

Ten Murderous Tales

Brindley Hallam Dennis

Copyright © 2015 Brindley Hallam Dennis

All rights reserved.

ISBN:1539156788
ISBN-13:9781539156789

CONTENTS

	Acknowledgments	i
1	Stump	1
2	Cat Alley **Blues**	6
3	Darkbury	11
4	Contributory Culpability	22
5	Consommé	27
6	The Rage	33
7	Talked Out	42
8	The Turkey Cock	52
9	Flowers	57
10	Wheel Ruts in the Snow	64

ACKNOWLEDGMENTS

First Foot, Consommé, The Rage & Wheel Ruts in the Snow have been performed by Liars League London, and can be found in performance on their website

Cat Alley Blues is available as a digital download on CUTalongstory

The Turkey Cock was included in the 2015 HISSAC Winners anthology, in an Inktears Showcase anthology & in The Carrot#2. You can see BHD reading it on Vimeo at BHDandMe

Stump won 3rd prize in a Sentinel Literary Quarterly competition.

Talked Out was an Inktears prize winner and was included in a Showcase anthology

1 STUMP

For a moment the birds had fallen silent, and the bony fingers of the trees had ceased their brittle tapping. A breeze had died, and cloud shrouded the face of the sun, stripping warmth from the air. A figure passed out of the shadows beneath the pines, taking Wynright by surprise. The man was heavily built and wore his sandy coloured hair cut short with a parting on the right hand side. He had on a plaid coat of some stiff fabric. It came down to below his hips and could have concealed a holstered weapon. He made Wynright think of lumberjacks, but that may also have been the proximity of the trees.

Hello. He spoke in a perfectly normal English accent that you might have heard anywhere in Norfolk, but the voice was as thin as cheese wire.

Wynright smiled, to put the man at ease, and continued to lace up his walking boots, as if unconcerned. He was perched on the ledge at the rear of the car with the hatchback swung up over his head. The stranger stepped in closer and returned the smile.

You're thinking of going into the woods, he said.

Yes. Wynright pulled the lace tight on his second boot and stood up, conscious of the proximity of the man.

It's very wet in there. The stranger pointed down to his own boots, which were very wet, but perfectly clean. They were yellow leather, industrial looking, probably safety boots with steel toe caps, and quite new. The bottoms of his trousers were soaked too. Wynright almost said, You look as if you've been paddling, but thought better of it. The trousers, blue denim jeans, looked new too. In fact, Wynright thought, nothing that the man was wearing looked as if it had belonged to him for long. It was as if he had kitted himself out anew for his trip into the woods.

It would be drier on the coastal path, the man said, and he raised one hand and pointed to the far side of the road. The sun will have dried the ground out there, he said, adding, I guess.

Wynright suppressed the urge to tell him that he had no intention of walking on the coastal path, saying instead, in the same careful voice, Yes.

You can see the Boston Stump from the coastal path, the man said, on a clear day. The Boston Stump is a famous landmark: like a legless, armless torso, from which the head has been severed. The man assumed that Wynright would know that. He waited, but not for Wynright to comment in reply. Wynright waited too. He did not like the idea of the stranger standing behind him while he turned back to the car boot. Was that what the man was waiting for him to do?

Maybe I should go that way, he said, and the man nodded.

That might be better, he said. He shifted uneasily from foot to foot in his wet shoes.

Is that your car? Wynright asked. There was only one other car on the car park; a four by four with a cased spare wheel hung on the door at the back.

Yes, the man said. He took a pace further away and Wynright felt the tension ease. I'd better be going, the man said. He took another pace away, as if he were reluctant to turn his back on Wynright, and he moved crab-wise across the compacted gravel of the car park towards the four by four, not taking his eyes off Wynright's face. A few paces from the vehicle he de-activated the locks, glancing towards the four by four briefly to assure himself that the warning lights had flashed. You would not have expected him to be the nervous type.

Wynright imagined himself going into the woods and then

returning only to find the man still there, waiting for him, questioning why he had not taken the shoreline path after all. He imagined the man becoming agitated, aggressive even, inquisitive as to what he had been doing.

I'd better be going too, he said, stepping away from the hatchback.

In one swift sequence of movements the man opened his car door, slipped into the driver's seat, with his clean wet boots and soaked trouser bottoms, closed the door behind him and started up the engine. Wynright thought he heard the clunk of the door locks re-activating. Then the vehicle moved backwards under a gentle pressure of the engine, turning as it went, to bring the bared teeth of the radiator grill facing towards him, and then it moved forward and turned aside, the silhouetted head of the man nodding as it passed, leaving the car park.

Wynright listened, mentally following the sound of the engine as it growled along the narrow country road, jolting over the level crossing, and accelerating away, changing down for the sharp bend before the climb up the embankment onto the dual carriageway. When it had merged into the hum of the distant, disconnected, traffic, he relaxed.

Suddenly the car park was graveyard quiet, into which silent pit the single notes of bird calls fell one by warning one. The shadows had thickened along the margins of the woodland. Wynright turned back to the hatchback and reached into the boot. He heaved out the black plastic bin-liner and the spade.

2 CAT ALLEY BLUES

The brighter the sunlight, the deeper the shade.

The roads diverge beyond the bridge. The wedge of land between is crowded with dog-leg lanes and alleyways. Tall and narrow buildings jostle for air space above and obstruct the thoroughfares below. No straight line crosses from one side to the other. All paths are forced to twist and turn; down side-alleys, beneath brick arches and along dark tunnels, following ways that subtly, secretly conspire to turn the traveller back, or lead to dead ends. In that labyrinth of doubt and uncertainty you surrender all sense of forward motion, exist in a nightmare where the world moves around you, but you are fixed in unspecified space.

No wheeled vehicles pass through the maze. Police cars cannot get in. Pursuing officers lurch to a halt and wait for back up with dog-handlers. Eye-in-the-sky helicopters are useless above the narrow, overhung gorges between the buildings. A Hell's Angel, riding through on his Harley, for a dare, had emerged in a shopping trolley, and wearing only a floral print frock.. The bike was never seen again. Emergency services have no contingency plans.

He had spent the day in the city, and had dressed to kill: dark suit, black bowler, rolled brolly, and brief-case, despite the bright spring sunshine. Business had been dead, but you only need to make a killing every now and then. Doubts, it was apparent to observers – of whom there were several – had assailed *Him*. Here was a stranger not going where *He* wanted to go.

You looks lost, mate, a tall athletic man in a short leather jacket over blue jeans and trainers spoke. *He* gave an address on the far side of the other main road. The man shook his head and sucked his teeth. That was one posh part of town, the man knew.

You is on the wrong road entirely, sunshine, the man said, waving his arms in the air, which made the heavy bling upon his wrists and around his neck sparkle in the eager sunlight. The man stepped in protectively closer. You should've taken the other fork. The man held out two fingers of one hand, and tapped one of them with the forefinger of his other.

He uttered a mild, gentlemanly expletive. The man nodded, as if in agreement, and pointed to the wall of old buildings with its cracks and pits of alleyways and its cracked and filthy windows.

You needs to pass through to the other side, the man said. A shadow of doubt crossed *His* face, though the sun still chuckled down upon them. You is in need of a guide and you is in luck, for I am going that way myself.

He glanced at the man. Not only tall and muscular, but tattoos from the backs of his hands scuttled up beneath his black leather cuffs, and the ropes of gold with which he was adorned, if of truly precious metal, must be worth their weight in themselves. The bulge beneath his jacket might be a pistol, or a cosh, or then again simply a wallet stuffed with cash.

Lead on, my friend, *He* said, having decided that the man would do. The man glanced from left to right and then, choosing the darkest and narrowest of the alleyways plunged, out of sunlight, into the gloom.

This way, the man said.

The alleyway was lined in old brick, brown as skin. It smelled of burnt fat. A brick arch lifted over their heads to let them in and a chipped sign, black letters on a pale background, said 'Dog Lane'. *He* followed. The man moved like a cat, keeping to the centre of the footway, his shoulders slightly stooped as he passed through. The cold grey air pressed down upon them. At a junction the man paused briefly, then pistoled a finger and led off to the left. *He* raised an eyebrow and gave a nod before following. Windows were blinded with dust and old fabric on which the colour had darkened like dried blood. The man looked back, glancing down at *His* brief-case.

Keep hold of that, the man said.

I will.

The sounds of the main roads had faded behind them, and the sun could not lean forward so far as to see down more than to the rooftops and the upper floors. They walked in shade and shadow. The smell of burnt fat had mingled with other smells: a smorgasbord of odours, sharp, sweaty, pungent, sour, heavy and insistent. Gobbets of music and of undigested words were thrown from upstairs windows and fell upon them as if from upended pails. Walls of stone and brick leaned in on them. Old doorways were closed against them. They twisted and turned, left, right, left again, left once more, across a small courtyard into which the sun peeped down almost as far as their heads, and where dirty water ran in a gutter from an unseen source to hidden drains. Then into darker gloom and a narrower alley, the man's head turning, left to right, picking up the clues of his intended track.

You know when you are going deeper in, even though you don't know the way. A cat, crouched at a grating into which its prey had wriggled, watched them go with dark, knowing eyes. They made another turn and followed a curving wall to stop dead inside a chimney of rising brickwork onto which no windows gazed.

Bugger! The man said, standing with his hands on his hips and staring upwards.

An easy mistake, *He* said, but here's fine. *He* had already opened the brief-case and taken out the captive-bolt gun, which he pressed into the man's dark hair.

3 DARKBURY

Francois said I should turn it into a story.

I said, Francois, how come you have a French name? He wore dreadlocks, and spoke with a London accent.

He said, John, how come you have a Jewish one?

I had to admit, he'd got a point. I said you can't be held responsible for what your parents called you, and he extended his arms, palms upwards, out to both sides, and raised his shoulders.

Besides, he said, French was the official language where my parents came from. I said, yeah, it was here too, until the rest of us invented English.

That brought us back to the story.

I said, not enough happens, in the story, to make a story.

So add some stuff, he said.

What sort of stuff? I asked.

He said, how about a McGuffin to begin with?

I said, no thanks, I'm on a diet. Only kidding.

Darkbury was in the north of England. It was perched above a steeply falling slope, studded with outcrops of old red sandstone, that slipped down to a fast flowing dark-water stream. The place was constructed of the same gritty, blood-red stone, which darkened to black when wetted. Behind the house, where the slope flattened out but kept on rising to a whale-backed false horizon, someone, many years before, had planted beech and oak trees, which now towered above what remained of the building.

It was an impressive house, even in its ruin. One wing was almost gone. The roof had vanished, slates, stone and timbers having been robbed out for use elsewhere. The walls were, as they say, showing like rotten teeth, sticking up here and there, the bevelled edges of old mullions and doorways adding a romantic charm. The middle section was complete, but unlived in, for the roof leaked and dampness was eating the walls. Curtains and carpets and soft furnishings would darken and take on a musty smell within weeks. Besides, no-one had added gas or electricity to it. Cracks had opened up, like intricate routeways, between the blocks of which the bare walls were built.

Rufus lived in the other wing, the one that teetered over the edge of the gorge. Two great sandstone buttresses, like sabre-tooth fangs, stabbed down into the bedrock from the corners of this pile, and above them a modern picture window, for which planning permission must have involved bribery and corruption on a massive scale, looked out across the void. He had kept this part up to standard, even adding a rudimentary form of central heating. The room with the picture window occupied the whole of the width of the building, and above it were two side by side bedrooms. Behind, on the ground floor, was a tiny kitchen, and above that, on the first floor back, was a tiny bathroom. A natural fissure in the rock had been widened at the rear of the kitchen and led down into a square stone cellar in which Rufus stored several bottles of wine and port. The stairs were lethal, because he had also installed a fridge and a freezer down there, to which he had run in a cable that snaked down the steps themselves, held in place, more or less, by electrician's tape, glued to the sandstone, most of which had, or was about to, come loose.

I'll get around to fixing that, Rufus frequently said.

Rufus was in his late forties, or early fifties. It was difficult to tell from looking at him, so one listened for clues in his conversation. References to Punk Rock suggested he had been an afficiando at the age when that would have been appropriate.

The story doesn't really concern Rufus though, but centres on a scullery maid called Jesse Norman who worked at the house when Darkbury was still intact and fully occupied. Some McGuffin, eh?

In those days the steep gardens were immaculately kept, and narrow paths, stairways in effect, zig-zagged down the slope, winding their way around and, in one or two dark and gothic places, actually through the stone outcrops that kept the building out of the water.

The stream itself was as nature had made it. No attempt had been made to control or amend its course, or its wild ways. It gathered its waters, from a series of rivulets and springs that meandered to a stone lip through a mile or two of rolling pasturland and meadows above the house. At the lip it paused briefly and then flung itself down some twenty feet of slab-rock waterfall into a plunge pool below. Out of this it spilled and bubbled along the crack of some natural fault line or tilted bedding plane for the quarter mile or so of the gorge upon the precipice of which Darkbury stood. After storms, debris and fallen branches, sometimes whole trees, would ledge among the rocks, only to be swept away in later deluges. The waterfalls pounded incessantly, and if you stood on tip-toe and were motionless, you could feel the vibration through the stone flagged floors.

At the lower end of the gorge the outcrop subsided into the surrounding fields and the stream became placid once again, running through yet more water meadows above which flies rose and fell on invisible strings in the heat of summer afternoons. In the winters, icicles hung like dripping knives from the sandstone edges and the waters ran secretly beneath opaque white ice-sheets.

The village, the church-spire of which could be seen above a line of trees that marked the end of the meadows, lay perhaps two miles downstream, but in its fat and lazy valley it might as well have inhabited an entirely different world. To the villagers, Darkbury was a name of evil repute. Not that Rufus or his wife were held in disrespect or loathing. Rufus had moved in only a few years before, when already two thirds of the place had fallen or had been abandoned. But the name of the house was resonant with earlier wrongs.

You know, he said, there's a room, in the middle part, that the locals call the Chamber of Terror. What do you think of that?

It was a gaunt, tall room. Gloomy, even in the brightness of days, for the roof was not off, and though the mullioned windows stood unglazed and open to the skies, the shadow of their carved stones seemed always to out-darken the lightness of the sun, and as evening came on, and the shadows of the trees reached out with threatening arms to enclose the house, the darkness in that room, of all, seemed to rise more quickly.

It's said, Rufus explained, that young Jesse had some sort of affair, with one of the children of the house, which ended rather badly, and in here. Oh, yes! He would say, the locals have considered this place to be haunted for generations. That's when you'd take a look around to see what it was standing behind you, and find nothing there.

Of course, he would add, they weren't children in the sense of children. They weren't minors, at the time of the events. It was one of those class-crossing affairs, that always ends badly for the servant class. But what made this all the more shocking was that young Jesse, and here, whichever room he was telling the story in, Rufus would look around him as if cautious about being overheard, young Jesse had her affair with one of the daughters of the family.

If he were telling it in the room itself, in the Chamber of Terror, he would walk to the window and look down. Standing beside him, the view was frightening. The picture window in the lived in part looked out over the gorge, but this central section of the house, which stood back from the edge, revealed another secret: a crevice that ran back at right angles from the main channel of the stream, narrow at its top, and narrowing as it descended. How deep it was is difficult to say, but there was water in the bottom of it, as black as old blood, and who knew how far beneath that dark surface the crack ran on? Even standing there, in the light of day, generations later, the pull of the crevice could be felt, like a real, though invisible pair of hands, dragging at your shoulders, pulling them down towards the abyss. Tangles of what looked like pale sticks were wedged in the tightness of the rock near that deep down water surface, and pale round stones, like eggshells, were caught among them..

Even birds get caught in there sometimes, Rufus said. They fly in after insects and become disoriented by the narrow sides. They break their wings against the moss, against the stone. They fall awkwardly. Sometimes they struggle for hours, sometimes for days. It is remarkable what resilience, what endurance, even the smallest of creatures have, when trapped in there, wedged, beyond hope of saving.

Of course, birds cannot have hope. They have no concept of a future in which there is anything to be hoped for. Without knowledge of a future you cannot have hope. Cats, or dogs, he thought, were different, and would cry for rescue.

It drives you mad, eventually, listening to them, he said. And some nights, when foxes are abroad, or hunting birds, you will hear them calling, or rabbits. Rabbits are especially noisy in their dying. Animals are always falling into the crack, especially young ones, and when you hear them, their cries echoing like that, you cannot help but think, help but remember, imagine. The old man of the house used to sit in here, Rufus said, staring into the gully. It fascinated him. He was the one that drove them to it, the two girls, when he found out.

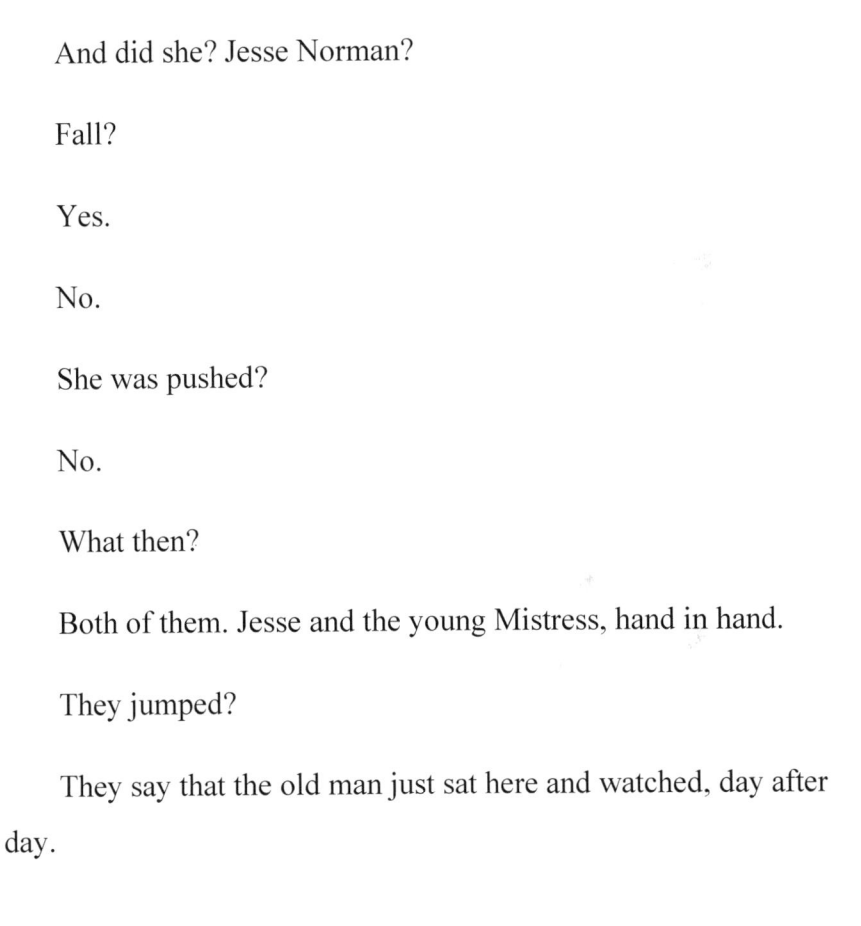

And did she? Jesse Norman?

Fall?

Yes.

No.

She was pushed?

No.

What then?

Both of them. Jesse and the young Mistress, hand in hand.

They jumped?

They say that the old man just sat here and watched, day after day.

Rufus stares. At the crevice. At his listeners. At the bare, damp walls of the Chamber of Terror.

Bats have taken up their residence in the roofspaces. Children, and young people, it is said, can hear them calling. Animals, it is thought, might do so. They fly around the building at twilight and dusk, into the darkness of night, in and out of the old defenestrated windows, into the narrow confines of the crack, which holds for them no fears, no dangers, no memories.

Francois said, you could make a meal of the affair itself. Hands moving beneath their gowns; lips kissing lips; the sensual disrobing. They had to be dressed and undressed in those days, the aristocracy. Couldn't do it for themselves.

Same these days, I said.

The slow dawning of recognition, of desire. The guilt, at the awareness. Then, the realisation that it afflicted, if that is the right word, them both.

That's not it though, I said.

Not what?

Not the story.

But it would give you more wordage.

Still not a story though.

You could play it all out, every last sexual encounter.

But why?

People like to imagine these things. You give them the chance, without it being pornographic.

I thought you said play it all out?

Not pornographic though, just sensual, erotic, and lots of it.

I still don't think there'd be enough.

Well, then add another bit on at the end, like the McGuffin.

What's that called, when you do it at the end?

No idea.

4 CONTRIBUTORY CULPABILITY

A few years ago I took a cottage in West Cumbria for a week to get some peace and quiet while I worked my way through a large number of documents. I'd been called in as a specialist by the legal team of a multinational that was defending itself against a negligence claim. Finding the smallest shred of evidence to suggest that the so-called victims have contributed to the disaster can save you thousands in damages, tens of thousands, millions even, if it's a class action.

The cottage was one of three old quarrymen's cottages sitting on a hillside beyond Rowrah in the back of end of nowhere, where the remains of old railway lines wind their way between the rounded foothills of the English Lake District. I worked long hours that week, breaking off for a sandwich at lunchtime, and driving down to the local pub for supper, and then doing another couple of hours before I turned in. One treat I allowed myself was a brisk walk in the mornings, after dawn, but before the sun had crested the curved summit of the hill behind the cottage.

I'd walk down the lane to where an old railway line crossed it, and then turn right onto the trackbed, which followed the curve of the hillside for about half a mile until it crossed the footpath that led back up the hill and onto the lane where the cottages stood. The remains of an old pair of buffers stood near the lane crossing, and down by the footpath there was the stump of an old finger post mounted on a slab of concrete in the shape of a cross set into the ground, that once would have shown the slight increase in angle of the descending incline. It was a pleasant walk, but something unsettled me as I reached the outermost point of the curve. There was a dark and tangled patch of briar there which for some reason seemed to contain a veiled threat. I could sense it pressing against my back as I walked away from it on that first morning, and on the second the feeling intensified to the degree that I imagined I could feel a cold breath against my neck, upon which the hairs rose.

On the Wednesday morning I could feel the unease growing even as I approached the place, and a sensation almost of panic hit me as I passed close beside it. Walking away, it was as if cold hands grasped me by the shoulder blades, and I had an unreasonable terror that if I were to turn around I would glimpse momentarily the black face of an approaching wall before it swept me away. On the Thursday, I chose to walk behind the cottage, up onto the low brow of the hill, beyond which the sun blazed in a clear blue sky and the distant mountains above Ennerdale were bright and cheerful. I told myself I had been a fool to have such wild imaginings, and on the last morning went down to the railway line once more.

I took with me a thick walking stick which I found among a selection in a tall pot by the front door, and when I reached the patch of briar I beat it down, determined to prove to myself that there was nothing there to fear. And neither was there, but only a coil of old wire and two stone slabs, though smaller than that of the finger post, and showing no signs of what they might have been. I was standing back to admire my handiwork when a voice spoke.

Thee's up at cottages, esta?

An old man had appeared, skinny, dressed in an old boiler suit and an oil-stained cap. He must have come up from the footpath. He was a dog walker, and had with him an equally ancient Irish Setter that looked at me with uncomprehending and incomprehensible eyes, and wagged a ragged tail like a faded red flag.

Yes, I said. I'm walking the circuit. I waved the walking stick around the ellipse of my morning stroll.

Thee's nut the fust, he said. He nodded back the way I'd come. There wuz a crossin' keeper wunce ower. Thee can see t'footings uv his owd cottage, if thee looks hard enow, up beside t'crossin'. He lived theer wi' 'is twa dowters. Thi niver wuz gates, but 'e'd cum aat at whistle wi' is red flag an' stop traffic if there were owt, while train passed. Thi were nowt but l'al trains, just a rake a' two or three wagons, full o' ore from mines up on't crags.

Fascinating, I said.

Folks didna fuss ower much back then, he said.

About what?

Abaht rules and regulations. The old man broke into a grin. They used to lie up wagons, driver an' fireman, in yonder cutting, uv a dinner time. He pointed back up beyond the lane crossing to where the trackbed curved up out of sight between the overgrown banks of an old cutting. They'd stick an' auld sleeper under t'wheels. Theer wus no brake van on sick a l'al train. Then they'd drift injun, light, a mile or two te next cuttin' an' leave it simmerin' while they nipped ower field t't Curren Arms fer a quick pint.

I knew that pub. It was the one I went to for supper.

Then back up an' hitch wagons and on theer way agin.

Why didn't they take the wagons with them? I asked.

Cuttin' next t't pub was too short for wagons, but thee could hide injun, and smoke'ud vanish in amang trees, even in winter, them being conifers.

Clever! I said.

Ay, canny buggers they wuz. He gave me a sly look. They'd giv young lassies a ride too, frae crossin' keeper's cottage to footpath yonder, wun yow tek. He swung round to face downhill. Keeper's dowters. Bright young things they wuz. They'd cum owt on 'twhistle an' jump in cab, and out agin at path, an' walk back ower hill, like you does.

I shook my head, wondering what else he might say. I had no idea how old the girls had been.

Cum the day, thi forgot ti put the sleeper up agin wheels, or mebbe set it wrang, an' wagons started to roll, silent as mist, and slow as last light, in't beginning, gatherin' pace as thi went. Driver an' fireman had barely got up bank when they heard crash of t'wagons 'ittin' stondin' injun. Fust wagon were smashed up and next two climbed ower t'wreckage, fillin' cuttin' wi broken timber and fractured metal an' spilled ore. Engine shot off on its own, all the way ti junction, wheer it came off at catch point protecting main line.

Amazing, I said.

Aye. Them twa buggers made up story about fust wagon comin' off and them jumpin' for they's lives. Woulda gotten away wi'it mebbe an' all, wer't nat fer two gals. He paused and glanced up the hill to where the sun was climbing at last above the false horizon, and I shivered.

Thi'd been tardy gittin' out ti sound o' whistle that mornin' and missed theer ride. Thi could see injun steamin' away down round bend, so they decided to follow arter, waalkin' dahn centre a' tracks.

5 CONSOMMÉ

If I had realised that Dr. Hemstitch had been dead for several years by the time I met him I would have been less enthusiastic about allowing him to kiss my hand. In fact he seemed remarkably active for a man of what I took to be his age, and it never crossed my mind that I might be saying hello to a corpse. He seemed so cheerful, which of course, in hindsight, was no surprise.

My dear, he said, in that deep resonant voice, how delighted I am to meet you. I was flattered, I admit, having entirely misinterpreted the reason for that delight.

The touch of his hand was firm and reassuring, reminding me of my dear, departed father's. His skin, though somewhat cool and dry, was not what one could call deteriorated in any sense of the word. His eyes sparkled with what seemed, and of course was, an unnatural light. Had I paused a moment or two longer on the doorstep, I have wondered since, might I have seen through that veneer of vitality, to the seething cauldron of corruption within that fuelled it? Perhaps. But as it was, the storm, had driven me, like Brad and Janet I suppose, to seek shelter at the house, although unlike Janet, I had no Brad upon my arm. Now the storm played its hand again, driving me across the threshold with such a flash of lightning that the forked image was burned into my brain, and with a crash of thunder, so close upon its heels that I thought the sky itself must be disintegrating above us. A distinct smell of sulphur lingered in the air as the echoes reverberated about the house.

Of course, you, from the comfort of your chair, may wish to tell me that had I paid more attention, to the good doctor, and before that to the house itself, I would not have found myself in the position in which I eventually did! Let me tell you though, that the rain, which had entirely overcome the efforts of the car's windscreen wipers to disperse, had doubled and re-doubled its efforts, to drive me towards my fate as soon as I had left the vehicle. Besides, there was a feverish anticipation in the good doctor that I could not resist the kindling of.

And who would judge a house by its elevations, and ornamentations, any more than a book by its covers? It was not some modern carbuncle upon the landscape, but a confection of late Victorian Gothic, with spires and turrets, and mullioned windows, shuttered against the weather with stout oak panels through which the yellow light of candles and perhaps log fires, flickered intermittently, rugs of black fur rolling like lovers before them.

As I stumbled forward Doctor Hemstitch gathered me into his arms with an affection that seemed almost wholly fatherly, and guided me into the hall. I must confess, I found the sweet scent of leather and tobacco attractive. The door swung to behind me with a dull thud, and I realised for the first time that we were not alone. A dry stick of a man, upon whom a threadbare suit of dark cloth hung like flesh upon the bone, was standing beside the door. He advanced toward me now with an odious smile, and as the whiff of sulphur died upon the air, another, darker, ranker, almost acrid smell, replaced it. I was sure that it emanated from this skeletal individual.

Raising an imperious palm my host stopped this apparition in its tracks. Not now, Cameron, he said, without explanation, and I felt his other palm pressing against the damp silk at my spine, as he guided me towards the open door of what I assumed must be some sort of reception room.

Not merely for reception. This room awaited an intimate tête-à-tête, a rendezvous-a-deux, an assignation amoreuse. A small round table draped with a heavy cloth scalloped and embroidered at the edge, and set for an elaborate meal, with crystal glasses, fine china, and bright, polished silver cutlery, stood a little way off from a shallow tiled fireplace in which an almost perfect flame burned seemingly without consuming the wood upon which it fed. Beside this table two elderly but comfortable looking chairs of plum-red plush upholstery invited our recline.

Are you expecting company? I asked, thinking perhaps that my arrival might inconvenience him.

Only one whose name I am yet to hear, he said, with old-fashioned gallantry.

Chloe, I replied, feeling myself slip into that comfortable, commanding submission against which intellect, and my mother, had warned me.

Chloe, the good doctor repeated, and he gazed with rapt compassion upon me and drew me into the room where he invited me to sit.

It is strange, is it not, he said, with barely the trace of an accent, that I should have asked Cameron to set a table for two, on such a night as this, no plans having been made, no invitations offered? Yet, as the storm grew, there grew with it my conviction, that a traveller would be cast upon my hospitality this night; and here you are, arrived almost in the nick of time. Indeed, so sure was I that one would arrive in need of food, that I had already instructed him that the time had come to prepare himself for our meal.

I'm not sure I understand?

The soup. He is ready. He clicked his fingers, and the cadaverous Cameron, who must have followed us from the hall, bowed briefly at the door and stepped back almost, it seemed with the air of one resigned to the performance of some last ritual long prepared for and inescapable.

Feeling at my ease, I unclasped my hair, and shook it free, to settle in folds like a discarded garment about my shoulders.

The room must have been warm, the air dry, for already, and I had been inside only a minute or two by then, my clothes seemed miraculously to have lost their wetness from the storm, and I must confess, that at no time in the whole of my previous existence had I felt so entirely at my ease as I did when sitting down to that momentous dinner. The Doctor was an unassuming, unpretentious host, yet as we dined I knew that he suppressed, with barely controlled excitement, the desires of a hunger that it was in my power alone to satiate.

The cuisine was superlative. The soup, of a flavour I had not encountered before, but which I have enjoyed many times since, was delicate and creamy, and it had been slightly foamed, as if it had been vigorously whisked the moment before serving. And I recall seeing Cameron's wrists, stretching from beneath the dark cloth as he served, and thinking that there could not be the strength in them to achieve such vigour. Of course, I told myself, there would be a cook, a jolly, rounded person, somewhere in the far reaches of the house. The entrée was a meat of such delicious tenderness, that it must have simmered slow and unctuous in its juices for a day or more, and the flavour, balanced with the perfection of a German wine, between that sickly sweetness, and acridity. Cameron, and I have to say that I did not entirely welcome this, seemed to linger by the table, having served this dish, waiting to reassure himself, by our approbation, that it was to our complete satisfaction, as if it were his own. Then with a weakening smile, the air seeming to waft unobstructed through the gaps between the buttons upon his jacket, he withdrew. The wine was dark, and red, and warming, as if mixed with some richer liquid of unknown provenance, and again, as Cameron served, tilting the crystal decanter above our glasses, I thought he trembled a little, and showed even paler in the dying firelight.

Who would have thought so rich a sweet could follow such a meal, in colour, texture, the aroma of burnt sugar and decay. Cameron, or what was left of him, seemed almost invisible within the ragged suit as he left us for the last time.

Death feeds on life. The Turks, it was said, back in the days of turreted castles and unbridled tyrants, would lash their living prisoners to the corpses of the slain, thigh to thigh, chest to chest, mouth to mouth, and see the living, inevitably, consumed by the dead. Good Doctor Hemstitch, as he served a golden honeyed after dinner wine, which he himself had fetched from some unknown vessel in another room, for Cameron was finished now, he told me, we are either eaten from without, or from within.

6 THE RAGE

Richard Meinhertzhagen, the famous soldier naturalist, said that if men do not hunt and kill animals frequently a rage will build up inside them that will lead, inevitably, to them desiring to hunt and kill other men.

Jeb had the face in the focus ring of the telephoto lens. It was a turnip face, red and blotchy with excitement and unbalanced diet. Weather had beaten it over the years, made the skin coarse and tough, drawn lines against the eyes; not of laughter, but of wincing into wind and rain, of squinting into light. The hunt follower's tight mouth was loosened by laughter now, like that of an ill-disciplined child falling on presents. As it turned towards him, filling the frame, the spittle on its lips was crystal clear in the cross hatching.

"What the fuck are you playing at?"

The voice was harsh and angry, and because his own face was pressed so tightly against the view finder Jeb did not associate it with the face that he was watching. He drew in the sleeve of the telephoto, trying to keep the focus, but the man was striding across the mud so quickly that he became a blur of green and brown.

"Hey! You with the camera!"

Jeb lowered the camera, a small fist of alarm suddenly hammering against his ribs. He was only a pace away, already reaching out with hooked fingers.

"Give us that you fucker!"

Jeb stepped back, shocked, defenceless. Mud sucked at his boots. The man slipped too, rolled sideways, like a small boat under a puff of wind. Jeb felt the hard bar of the stile jolt against his hip, and putting one hand out to steady himself, rolled backwards over the way he had come, like a hurdler re-played in reverse. He held the camera high in his other hand as his feet slipped and slithered to find a grip on the grass verge.

The man was at the stile, grabbing for his arm, preparing to haul himself over, breathing hard.

"Hold still you bastard."

"It's all right!" Jeb said hastily, as if that might make it so.

He stepped back, holding the camera away.

"Just give us the fucking camera."

"No fucking way man. I've got a right to take pictures. This is a public right of way.

They looked at each other. Then Jeb turned and ran for it. Let the old bugger catch him if he could.

Jeb ran as fast as he could, holding the camera tight against his chest. He ran uphill, between stone walls. Water coursed down, streamlike, puddling where cattle and tractors had made ruts. His heart beat against his chest like tiny ineffectual fists. He clutched the camera, as if he were being towed along behind it.

Jeb did not look back. The open gate on the skyline where the track spilled out onto the hillside danced before him like the image in a hand held camera. He could hear the sound of feet behind him. They pounded the ground like the pulses pounding in his ears. They were gaining on him. There must be a mob of them, all joining in the chase. He dared not look round. He gasped for breath, ran faster.

The drumming grew louder, closer. He worked the memory card out of the camera with his free hand and let the SLR fall to the ground. He could get another. The insurance would cover it. But the pictures were special. Isn't that what a journalist would do? Sacrifice the camera, but keep the pictures.

But the drumming kept up, almost level with him, almost above him. A shadow fell on the side of his face. He glanced across, veering towards the far side of the track. A horseman, looking straight ahead galloped past on the other side of the wall. Others followed. He saw their tall bodies rise as they jumped the last wall before the open hillside. He stopped running and threw himself down onto his knees, looking back. The track was empty behind him. Ahead, the horsemen were scattering across the hillside. They were not after him.

He laughed and shook his head, tried to slow his breathing. Silly bugger, he thought. They probably hadn't even seen him. Tension drained from him. What was there to be afraid of? What could the fat old bastard have done? It was because he was not used to violence. Not like that, face to face.

His grandfather, who had lived through the war, said people had lost the ability to cope with violence. They were not used to it anymore. That was why they feared it so much. They had no experience by which to judge the degree of threat. He nodded at the wisdom of his rationale. A wave of sympathy for the hunt follower washed over him. You could hardly blame him for being upset, what with hunt saboteurs and animal rights activists. How was he to know that Jeb was a portrait photographer, and just curious about faces? He hadn't even known there was a hunt on. He'd just been out walking, following the public right of way.

Jeb took a deep breath. His hands were still shaking. Sunlight slanted down through the bare branches of a tree and sparkled on a fallen leaf by his foot, bronzed with rotting, lacquered with dew, like a small curved brooch that someone had dropped. Goodwill settled on him like warm spring sunshine.

He walked back to where the camera lay. His legs wobbled like a new born lamb's. The camera looked up at him, solid, unperturbed. He bent to retrieve it. Then he saw the four by four, rocking slowly from side to side as it crawled up the track like a shiny black beetle.

At first he did not connect it with the man, but something in the steady, deliberate progress that it made through the mud released the fear in him again. It yawed and rolled, slipped sideways, and righted itself. The bright discs of the headlamps shifted from side to side like the eyes of a hunting animal.

He froze, his hand on the camera. The vehicle came on, slowly, determinedly, the moaning of the engine a warning growl. He could see the squat black shape of the driver behind the wheel.

He snatched up the camera and ran again, the tiny fist hammering at the back of his throat. He was already near the end of the track. It spilled onto the hillside in a tangle of wheel ruts, gathered itself and turned, following the fence line. He turned with it, as if he might go faster over the rutted surface than over open ground. A barn stood, stone-bright in the sunshine, the open doorway a black oblong. He plunged inside. The vehicle had not yet cleared the turn. The man would see nothing but the bare hillside when he turned that corner, Jeb told himself. It would be as if he had vanished.

The barn was tiny, windowless save for three slits high up in the back wall that glowed like vertical neon lights. Arrow slits, he told himself. Sunlight streamed in through the doorway, ran across the gravel floor, splashed against the metal spikes of some unrecognisable farm implement that leaned against the wall. Jeb threw himself down in the far corner, curling into the shadows like a dog beneath a table.

He could hear the growl of the Mitsubishi engine choke into silence; could see the oblong of brightness that the sun flung down through the open door. Onto that oblong fell the shadow of a man.

Jeb watched it move towards him. Then the hunt follower was standing looking down at him. He carried a heavy stick, cut from a branch of thorn, grey bark pustuled with raised stumps where thorns had been removed.

"Take it." Jeb said in a small voice, pushing the camera across the rough stone floor.

"Too late for that son."

He swung the stick down, a one handed blow that fell across Jeb's shoulder. Jeb could not believe that wood could feel so hard. He cried out. The blow had been half hearted, but the cry encouraged the man, and he struck again, this time towards the head. Jeb ducked and shielded himself with his arm. He could feel the skin on his forearm tearing, even through his coat. The man grasped the stave with both hands and swung again, reversing the movement and catching Jeb across the chest.

He caught the head, a sharp jarring sensation, like hitting an oversized cricket ball. Blood splashed against the grey stone wall. That made him pause, and he stood, looking on, breathing heavily, his heart pounding.

Jeb felt as if he were on fire, as if he rolled in flames. He could smell blood, taste it. The cessation of the blows made him glance up. He saw the man swaying, red faced, breathing hard, hefting the stick, preparing to strike again.

Then Jeb found in himself that rage of which Meinhertzhagen had written, and the hunt follower was no longer a man, but some vile horrifying insect that had taken him by surprise, and without reason or thought, he uncurled and flung himself forward in a blind fury of loathing and fear.

The movement caught the man by surprise, knocked him off balance and the two of them careered backwards across the floor. The man gave a gasp, air coming out of a bag, and a sharp curved tine of the piece of machinery burst out through his chest, glistening with blood, missing Jeb's face by inches.

They stood motionless, locked together, unbalanced, held up by the spikes onto which the man had been driven. He looked down, moving like someone trying to extricate himself from a sleeping partner whom he did not wish to disturb. Jeb loosened his grip, and pulled away. The man was standing at an impossible angle, his legs bent beneath him, his weight pushing him down further onto the spikes. A second tip nuzzled through the tweed of his waistcoat like the snout of a small rodent. He reached one hand behind him, feeling for the upright metal frame, trying to hold himself still. His eyes reminded Jeb of a bird he had found once, half disembowelled but still alive.

The man was still holding the stick. Jeb took it. The pain had abated, but the rage had not. He grinned, and saw fear rush into the man's eyes as he swung the knotted stick as hard as he could against his chest.

The sun was bright. A blackbird sang like a stream. Jeb closed his eyes and let the warmth play on his face. There was the faintest breeze, as soft as fingers against his cheek. He had never felt so light, so clear, and free. He felt as if, were it not for his heavy boots, he might drift off, like a spider borne on gossamer, flashing in the sunlight over the fields. He had never known such a feeling of peace; such a gentle, warm feeling of goodwill towards the world. It was all so beautiful, he thought, that he did not know whether to laugh or cry.

7 TALKED OUT

Writers have their season; a flowering, and then it's over. They run out of ideas, or memories, lose that 'visionary gleam'. There's nothing you can do for them then, except make them comfortable and wait for the end. That's what I needed to do for LJ.

His last novel had sold well, but that was on the back of previous good ones. The next one would flop. That was why we wouldn't be publishing the next one. Luckily, there was no sign of him writing it, so I wouldn't have to be the one to tell him. In fact, I had assumed it was so he could tell me that there wouldn't be one that he had asked for the meeting. In my experience writers fall into one of two categories – those who drink when they can, write that is, and those who drink when they can't. LJ, it turned out, was one of the latter.

We met after hours in my office, which was dry, but he brought his own bottle, which was already half empty. He set it down on the low table by the sofa, and seated himself next to it. I carried over a paper cup from the water dispenser and handed it to him.

This'll have to do, I told him. I don't have glasses.

That's OK, he said, taking it from me and half filling it.

I confess I was disappointed, and surprised. I'd thought up to then he might be one of that third type, the mythical ones who didn't drink at all.

He surprised me too when he spoke.

I've got a new story for you.

I sat down opposite him, and he began to tell it.

It's at the end of the sixties, maybe the early seventies, he said, and I've just left school.

It's a first person narrative, I said. What you've got to bear in mind with a first person narrative, is where will the protagonist be at the end? Where is he telling the story? When? And to whom? Especially if he's the one who gets murdered.

That's right, he said. He said, I decided to go to France. Kids were hitch-hiking all over Europe that summer. The weather was hot and sunny, but the French police had taken it into their heads to crack down on the hippies, and that had freaked out the drivers, who were getting stopped if they had anyone in their cars with hair longer than a foreign legionnaire's.

That's hard to swallow, I said.

Believe me, he said, it was. He said, so, anyway, lifts were hard to come by. I ended up walking east along the coast road from Calais.

You could put in some local colour, I said, about Calais. I'd camped in Calais about the time his story was set. There used to be a camp-site right on the sea front, next to the harbour. You had to walk across this bridge, a swing bridge if I remember, to get into the town itself. One of those little Deux Chevaux vans used to show up early every morning, peeping its horn, selling eggs and bread, and milk. The guy who drove it was very jolly, singing that Papa Joe song in broken English.

LJ was staring at me.

Never mind Calais, he said. He said, I walked for two days. I stopped even trying to get a lift. I'd left the coast road, and was veering inland. I crossed the border into Belgium on some minor road with no douanier. I was getting bored, but I'd picked up this stash, you know, of red Leb.

Isn't the drugs thing a bit out of your line? I said.

This was then, he said. He said, I got into this forest; some sort of plantation. Pine trees. I can still smell it, like disinfectant.

The heat brings it out, I said.

Yeah, he said. He said, and they'd been logging too. The cut wood was piled all along the track and there were great mounds of bark chippings.

Did they have de-barking machines back then, I asked. He ignored the question.

He said, I was high as a kite. I had no idea how much of the stuff to use, you know, to make a joint. It was my first time, and my last. I came across this little French car. You know the sort: roof like the cover off an old-fashioned pram, gear lever sticking out of the dashboard like an umbrella handle.

Deux Chevaux, I told him.

Whatever. Well, it was sitting there, on the side of the track. No-one with it, but it was open, and the keys were in.

Mm, I said, maybe a bit too contrived, too much of a co-incidence. I nodded my head, like a rear window dog. He shot me a look.

So, I got in and fired it up. I'd just passed my test, a couple of months before, but I'd never driven anything like that. Then I saw him. This guy in blue overalls running through the trees towards me. He was wearing a fucking beret. It must have been his car. He was yelling something, but I didn't know what. I knew what he meant though. Then I got the thing into gear, and we shot off the verge and onto the track. He stops dead, and then goes off running in the other direction. I should have paid more attention to that.

LJ lifted his two hands and stared down at them, turning the palms over as if searching for the next part of his story in the lines upon them. He had big hands, clumsy hands with thick stubby fingers. I used to wonder how he managed with mobiles, even the laptop keyboard.

Well, I went scooting down the track. It was like a cake walk. Can you remember them? We were bouncing around like there was no tomorrow, and I was laughing, because of the drugs, you know? Then I came round the bend, and there was the guy again, the guy with the overalls and the beret.

The beret's a good touch, I said. You need some detail like that, to identify the character immediately. He pressed on regardless.

He wasn't standing in the road, though. He was high up, on the seat of some big machine. There was no way round him.

I said, you can do the research; find out what they would have been using back then.

He said, sure. But, I hit the brakes, and the car stalled, and I got out. I was still laughing like crazy, and he got down off his seat and stood looking at me. He was built like a bull. Like one of those French cows, only the bull, you know, the big white ones. Short, and no neck, and he wasn't laughing.

You steal my car.

I said, hey man. That's they way we talked back then. I said, hey man, it's cool. There's no harm done.

You steal my car.

I held up my hands. I said, it's cool man. I said, it's just a joke, OK? I was still laughing, because of the dope, but he hadn't cracked a grin.

You steal my car.

I said, no way man. I said, I borrowed your fucking car. I said, no harm done, man, and he stepped up towards me.

He said, You steal my car, like he was some sort of fucking record stuck in the groove. You steal my car. You steal my car.

I said, no man. I said, it's cool. I borrowed the fucking car. I said, no harm done. Then he said. I get the police.

I was thinking, no way man. No police. I mean, there's no harm done. The fucking car is sitting there, right next to us. There's not a bump, a scratch, a dent on it, nothing, well nothing new. I mean. It's sitting there. What more does he want? And the police were fucking cracking down, man. They were cracking down, and I've got hair down to my backside and a bag of red leb in my rucsac the size of a small football. There's no way we're getting the police involved.

But he keeps on getting closer, and he's starting up again, you steal my car. Then he reaches out with both hands and grabs me by the shoulders.

LJ sat and stared at me, and I thought, it's not going to make a novel. A short story, perhaps, with some sort of twist at the end, but he'd have to work on the atmosphere, the setting, get in the heat of the sun, the dryness of the air, the sound of the pine trees clicking as they rubbed their brittle fingers together above his head, the shadows thrown down sharp against the sand.

So, what happens next, I said, and LJ swallowed, as if he'd taken a gulp from the cup, which in fact he hadn't touched. He glanced wildly from side to side, as if he was watching a wild bird that had got loose in the room behind me. But there was nothing loose in the room except him and me. There was nothing loose in the building. The cleaners had gone long ago.

That's when, he said.

When what?

When I grabbed him too, and LJ looked down at his hands again.

Go on, I said.

I strangled him, he said.

Is that possible? I asked. I remembered then, how LJ used to carry a tennis ball, which he'd squeeze in his hands. He told me once that if you practised hard enough, for long enough, you'd be able to entirely crush the ball in your fingers, and when he told me that I'd asked exactly the same question. Is that possible? And he'd pulled the ball out of his pocket and crushed it there and then, in his left hand, which was the one he used for writing.

It's possible, he said. He said, the guy had the thickest neck you ever saw. I could barely get my hands around it, but I got my thumbs up against his windpipe, and his beret fell off.

LJ was staring at me again and we sat there for what seemed like minutes, and it was silent except for the ticking of a clock somewhere behind me, and the smell of disinfectant that had seeped into the room from somewhere else.

Is that the end of the story? I asked.

He said, I needed to get rid of the body. I'd worked in the woods back home. I knew my way around a chain saw.

Your going to have the body cut up with a chain saw? I said. I was going to add, isn't that a bit clichéd, but LJ was looking shocked.

God no, he said. He shivered. I could never do something like that. He smiled one of those sly smiles that children sometimes have when they're feeling particularly pleased with themselves.

I got lucky, he said. There was a fallen tree, windblown. Without that I'd have been screwed, he said. I must have looked blank.

When they come down like that, he explained. They make a big hole, where the root plate sat. I dumped him in there.

But surely, that's not a very good hiding place, I said.

It is when you put the tree back on top of it, he said. Nobody would even know there had been a hole.

Sometimes an author can spend his whole life trying to get a particular story out. Some say D. H. Lawrence was like that. I often wondered if it were true of Cormac McCarthy. Authors like that go on plugging away at the same theme, trying to get it right. It doesn't matter if it's a best seller they've written, if it hasn't said what they were trying to say, they have to try again. Of course, it doesn't always work when they get there. When those stories come out they're often not the stories that anyone wants to hear. They're not the stories those writers should have been the ones to tell.

He said, when a tree's blown over like that, if it's still alive, and not been lying too long, the main root is like a spring. It's been bent over you see, and all it wants to do is to get back to it's normal shape. The only thing stopping it is the weight of the tree.

I said, as a plot device, that's intriguing, but hard to believe. He carried on.

All you have to do is cut the tree off, and the stump will swing back into place. Anything that's underneath will never be seen again. No-one's going to start looking underneath the trees for someone are they? They wouldn't think of that? Unless you've seen it happen, you wouldn't believe it.

There's another curiosity about writers, about stories. Sometimes you can talk a story out: tell it before you've written it. Then when it comes to the writing, you can't do it at all, or if you can, it writes out flat, uninteresting. It's as if, stories like that, having been told, don't need to be told again. They don't need to be written down.

I was beginning to worry that LJ might have told me too much already.

I'm not worried about that, he said.

What about fingerprints? I asked. What about DNA?

With no body, it was a missing persons file, not a murder hunt. DNA wasn't known about in those days anyway.

You only need the tiniest amount, I told him, to put you at the scene of a crime these days. I said, and you can get fingerprints off fingerprints these days, but he didn't seem impressed. I reached out and took a drink from the cup, which he still hadn't touched.

And does anybody ever find out, I asked him after a silence.

Not unless I tell them, he said.

8 THE TURKEY COCK

The taxi rank was tucked against the wall downhill from the station. Two women laden with shopping bags were climbing into the last taxi. Manx loitered awkwardly on the pavement, waiting for the next one to pull up. A little man with bird bright eyes followed him down and stood beside him.

You must be a clever bloke, the little man said, pointing to Manx's briefcase, and staring into his eyes.

Not especially, Manx said, feeling uncomfortable.

Oh, I'm sure you are, the little man said, still staring and stepping closer. I bet you're very clever indeed.

I'm just average, Manx said, smiling.

No, no, the little man insisted. I'm sure you're very, very clever. Why would you need one of those otherwise?

I might have my sandwiches in it, Manx said.

You see! You are clever. That's a very clever thing to say, in a situation like this. Why I bet you're clever enough to talk your way out of anything. He was standing so close now that Manx could smell the beer on his breath.

I don't know about that.

Now, me, I'm sure you'd think I was a stupid man, wouldn't you?

I'm sure you're not stupid.

Are you now? Are you really?

Manx said nothing more, but that was not enough. It had gone beyond the point of saying nothing.

I think that's what you think I am, the little man said, stepping up so close that he and Manx were almost touching. You think I'm stupid.

I think you're a bully, Manx said.

What?

I said, I think you're a bully. The little man took a pace back. I think you like to bully people with briefcases, because you think they'll let you.

You what?

I think you enjoy it.

The little man almost stopped, but he could not.

Who the fuck do you think you are?

No one important, Manx said, turning towards the next taxi, which had just pulled up beside them.

Don't fuckin' turn your back on me, the little man shouted, and he made a grab for Manx's sleeve.

And Manx dropped the briefcase, and pulled away, and grasped the little man by his wrist, and twisted it, so that the little man's arm was locked out straight; and Manx swung him round, and almost instinctively, for the first time since he'd done Judo as a kid, he swept his right foot round in a curve, like some fancy dance move, and took the little man's legs from beneath him; and as the little man fell, he turned him, using the twisted arm, which he now held firmly in both hands, as a lever.

And the little man landed face down on the pavement with his arm pulled taut and vertical behind him, and with Manx's foot pressed against his ribs.

And Manx knew for the first time in his life the wild joy of having another living thing entirely within his power, and the little man said, I'll fucking kill you, you bastard.

And Manx twisted the arm, putting the weight of his body behind it, and the little man screamed, and Manx felt something give, inside the little man's shoulder, and it reminded him of something but he could not remember what.

And Manx said, that's not what I want to hear, and the little man's eye, because the side of his face was pressed hard against the pavement, looked up at him like a bird's.

And Manx said, I want you to say, please don't hurt me, but the little man said, fuck you Jack.

And Manx pressed down with his foot and felt something brittle crack, and he pulled harder against the arm, and he could feel the little man's muscles tearing.

And the little man screamed and shouted please don't hurt me, but Manx said, it's gone beyond that now, and the little man's eye filled with tears and there was the sudden sour smell of faeces

And Manx said, you've shit yourself, but don't be embarrassed, because that often happens in situations like this, and the little man screamed more desperately than before.

Then the taxi driver, who'd witnessed it all, and had got out of his cab, which might in other circumstances have been a foolish thing to do, said, you've done enough, mate, don't you think?

And Manx looked at him, and knew he was right; but then he remembered what it was that twisting the arm had reminded him of, and he also remembered running away from a bully when he was at school, and he gripped the arm tighter and twisted it as hard as he could, and he felt it come away, just like the turkey leg had at Christmas, and the man on the ground stopped screaming, and heaved a great sigh, as if he really did regret everything, and Manx thought to himself, that however clever he was, he wasn't clever enough to talk himself out of this one.

9 FLOWERS

The detective looked in through the small grid of reinforced glass. He saw an elderly man sitting beside the plain wooden table, an empty chair at the far side. The man had short grey hair, neatly cut. He was round headed and with a still boyish face despite his years. He was studying the photograph that the detective had left with him, tilting it towards the dim light of a grubby slit window set high up on the opposite wall. The old man shook his head, not quite imperceptibly, which the detective took as his prompt to re-enter the room.

The photograph had been reprinted from an old newspaper cutting. It showed edges that were ragged, and a crease line down the middle separated the two women who knelt in the foreground, stripped to their underwear, heads shaven and bleeding. Behind them the faces of the crowd were blank, mindlessly curious rather than excited. The faces of the young resistance fighters were stern and businesslike.

What has this to do with Dedecker's Bar? The old man asked, looking up.

The detective, who had positioned himself at the far side of the table, but had not sat down, leaned forward and pointed to the top of the picture.

That's where it took place. You can see the sign board, above the heads of the crowd.

The old man nodded. It was a long time ago, he said, a lifetime.

The woman on the left, the detective said. Her name was Christine Jalbert. Perhaps you remember her?

The old man rubbed his palms against his face. Mais oui, he said eventually. Poor Christine. She was a victim of love. The other one, she was just a whore. She opened her legs for anyone, and opened her mouth too.

I'm not interested in the other one.

The old man smiled. No! Nobody was then either. He looked down at the photograph. But Christine; she had a German lover. A soldier. Some sort of specialist, a technician.

Tell me about Dedecker. He was a collaborationist?

Marc? Non. The Germans used his bar, but that was Okay. He kept his ears open, and his eyes, and he passed on what he could.

And you?

I was just a boy, barely sixteen then, small for my age. They would have taken me for the Arbeitskommando otherwise.

Slave worker?

I ran messages for the resistance. I had done so since I was twelve. The old man sat up straight. You have no idea what it was like.

No.

My uncle, he was a clerk, at the Town Hall. Not important, you understand, but he would not hand over the keys. The filing cabinets, the records of the workers? They were looking for Jews. They took him outside and shot him on the street.

I'm sorry.

You think this, he tapped the photograph, is an atrocity? The detective looked uncomfortable, as if he were the one undergoing interrogation. The old man continued. Let me tell you. Do you know the forest road? No? There are three stones, along the roadside. Even today they are kept clean, who by, I do not know, someone who remembers. One where the path leaves the trees. One at the crossroads. One outside the green house. I could tell you the names.

I'm sure you...

Wait! I have not finished. Eleven of them. The stones mark where they fell, between September 21st and 23rd, 1944. The town had been liberated by the end of the month.

I'm sorry.

Mort pour vous. That is what it says upon the stones, above their names. Mort pour vous. You understand?

I understand.

You do not. You cannot understand. And you want me to weep for Christine Jalbert?

It is not the fate of Christine Jalbert that concerns me.

Then who?

The detective sat down on the empty chair and produced a second photograph which he laid down upon the table and pushed towards the old man.

This is who I am interested in. The old man's face hardened. The photograph was taken in 1965, on his twenty first birthday, the detective said.

It showed a young man with close cropped blond hair and clean cut features. He was grinning into the camera. His teeth were unnaturally white, and perfectly straight.

Let me tell you what I think happened, the detective said. The kid would have been maybe twenty two, perhaps twenty three, depending upon how long it took him to get here. He came into Dedecker's Bar looking for someone. He ordered a drink, and Dedecker made small talk.

Go on, the old man said, leaning forward and gripping the edge of the table.

The kid was American, doing the hippie trail. Dedecker talked back in a phoney transatlantic accent he had picked up from Hollywood movies and from the G.I.s he'd met at the end of the war. Maybe Dedecker recognised him. He was the spitting image of his father, although he'd grown his hair long by then and had a beard of sorts. Or maybe the kid told him, my father was here in the war, imagining Dedecker would think he was some G.I.s kid. Maybe he told Dedecker that his pop had been a specialist, in the fifteenth army. Maybe he went on to tell him that his pop had had a girlfriend in the town. Maybe he told him that his pop had come back for her after it was all over. Maybe he told Dedecker how lucky he was to be alive, considering the way his mother had been treated. The detective pointed to the first photograph. You can see she is pregnant.

The old man relaxed against his chair back.

So where did you get these photographs? He asked.

The photograph of Arthur Muller came from the FBI. He's on their files as a missing person. The other we found in what used to be the cellar of Dedecker's Bar. When they bulldozed the site and re-developed it he must have thought he'd got away with it for good. But, as you know, they are re-building again, and with deeper foundations this time. The photograph was beside what was left of the body.

But Dedecker is dead, the old man said. He died years ago. Surely your case is closed? A sudden idea took him, and besides, Dedecker is not in this photograph.

No, *he* isn't, the detective said, and a silence fell into the room.

The old man laughed, and twisted his head towards the sky which showed, distant and blue, through the dirty glass of the slit window. When he looked back his face., rather than that of an eighty five year old, was that of a stern young man.

I have had a good life, he said. The detective said nothing. He came late at night, the old man said, Arthur Muller, just as I was closing the bar. By that time Marc was getting old and would go home early, leaving me to cash up and lock the place. He must have watched from the alleyway across the road, waiting until only I was left. Later I found his rucksack there between the rubbish bins. I knew him right away, of course, even with his long hair and that wisp of beard. He had his father's eyes. He was not looking for Dedecker. When he showed me photograph, I knew that.

Perhaps I could have talked him out of it. I have often thought so since but we learned to act swiftly in the resistance. I had killed a man before, in the last days of the war. He grew agitated, aggressive. It was not that he held me responsible for what happened to his mother that incited me. It was when he began to lecture me, to tell me that we were no better than they had been. Men are predisposed to talk or to fight.

The cellar was my only option. There were tools already there. I have needed to hide things quickly before. I think his family did not know what he intended. His father would have disapproved – that hair. His mother, Christine, would have talked him out of it. There were no return tickets in his papers. Nobody came looking for him. So many Americans were hitch hiking around Europe then. They were playing that song about San Francisco on the wireless. The Americans took many back with them, Germans, who they thought would be useful. The old man lowered his head and pressed his hands together. I burned his papers, the passport, anything that might identify him, even his clothes..

But the photograph? You folded it into a tin, left it beside the body, the detective said.

I could strip him of his clothes, of his documents, the old man said, but I could not bring myself to take away his story.

10 WHEEL RUTS IN THE SNOW

It's still snowing, but a thaw has set in sometime during the night. Sometimes it's hard to know when things change; that precise moment when the tide turns, or the season passes from autumn into winter; when the slope you are on tips from being in your favour to against it.

We weren't used to snow; not that amount of it. The cold froze our bones. The air scoured our throats, like neat whisky, all the way down. Sometimes I thought I'd lost the feeling in my legs, but that was not knowing better. They'd told us not to bring him back alive. He's an animal they said; vermin. That's how he thought of us as well. In those days it seemed normal, to think of them that way, to know that's how they thought of us.

Danny needed no persuading. God knew how many generations had passed down, with glacial deliberation, that unquestioned belief. God must have known. We were icebound in our certainties. Danny giggled like a big kid and pointed down at the tracks.

There's no way he can give us the slip, he said.

A white sun was like the moon through grey cloud. The glare made us screw up our eyes. We were tracking him along a country lane. There were tyre tracks in the snow, and in the untouched drift between them, his footprints. Danny must have been playing with himself, or touching something else in his pocket. I didn't plan on getting close enough to use anything so small that you could carry it in your pocket, so I kept the rifle unslung. The footprints were so clear you could almost read the maker's label on his boots. Danny said, he's never going to get away.

I thought, that's true. We've got him cold, and I was just making a joke to myself about not cold, but freezing, and I was thinking of dead meat, of frozen meat, swinging from meat-hooks in a refrigerated meat store.

That's when his prints stopped. They just stopped: left, right, left, right. Then nothing. Danny said, Jesus! But that wasn't it. We stopped too and just stood there, looking down at the virgin snow. That's what you call it, virgin, when it hasn't been fucked about with yet. I remember Danny's baby face with its big round astonished eyes.

Where did he go? He said.

Then it struck me what had happened. I said, he's stepped off into the tyre tracks. I even laughed. I even let him have the benefit of some respect, for a moment. Danny was still standing dumbstruck. Let's face it. Danny was a couple of coals short of a snowman.

I said, he's stepped into the tyre tracks, and Danny said, which side? I thought, you stupid kid, who cares which side? I should have thought better. I should have been thinking. It's no use asking questions unless you ask the right questions.

It felt cold all of a sudden up there on the hillside. Maybe it was us standing still. I thought, none of us is going to survive if we don't get a move on and catch up to him soon. That was the winter of sixty-three. There have been worse since, not just for snow.

I said, come on, and for some crazy reason we stepped into the tyre tracks too; me in front, Danny behind.

I couldn't see his tracks at all, not on either side. I was trying to work out, was it because the snow was compacted? Or did it mean a vehicle had passed over since he came this way? I kept telling myself, surely we'd have seen it? There were no tracks to show one having turned around. Could they have reversed back away from us?

They were good questions, but they weren't the right questions. Then Danny said, and I often wondered if he got the idea from one of those comic books he was always reading, what if he turned back?

I said, what? And that cold seemed to sweep in again, though there was no breeze whatsoever, and the whole place was as silent as the grave. There wasn't even the sound of distant traffic. Snow does that to the world.

I said, what? And Danny said again, what if he turned around, and then he turned around and started to look back down the lane.

And I thought, Jesus! Yes. That's what he did. But not turned around. He'd walked backwards a little way toward us, and then he took off across the fields, which we, following his easy footprints with our noses to the ground, entirely failed to notice. Then I got that feeling that I told you about: about not knowing the precise moment when things changed, but only knowing that they had.

And I thought, the bastard's behind us now. We were the ones being followed, and I looked around, and it seemed to me that this wasn't the sort of place you'd go to if you were trying to get away. It seemed to me that this was the sort of place you might lead somebody to if you needed to get them out into the open.

And I remembered a dead bird I found once in the snow when I was a kid, and the woods were entirely without colour, but only black and white, and even the bird was that dark shade of brown that seems to have no colour in it, and yet, there, right next to it on the pure white snow, without explanation, for the body seemed perfect, was the most beautiful splash of crimson you ever saw.

And I was remembering that when Danny said, oh! And I heard a crack like someone stepping on thin ice. And he slid down onto his knees, as if he were about to begin gathering snow with which to make a snowman. Then I felt a blow, as if someone had hit my legs with a heavy hammer, and then it was silent.

The cold got into my bones that day, and stayed, but Danny was stone cold, and the one we were tracking, he's long cold too, and thousands after him.

That's why I keep on looking out at the snow. It's falling heavily now, in big soft flakes, like pieces of wet tissue. I like to see it fall. I like the way it turns the world so silent. I watch from my window, every winter, and think back to that day. It's settling fast, but it won't last long. You could track anyone through snow like this, and for a long time that was what I planned to do, even in this chair, but somewhere, sometime, another thaw set in.

ABOUT THE AUTHOR

Brindley Hallam Dennis has published several collections of short stories and a novella. His work has been widely performed and published in magazines, journals and anthologies. Writing as Mike Smith he has published poetry, short plays and essays. His plays are available through Lazy Bee Scripts. He regularly writes for Thresholds, the International Post Graduate Short Story Forum. He lives in north Cumbria within sight of three mountain tops and a sliver of Solway Firth. He blogs at www.Bhdandme.wordpress.com

Second Time Around (short stories)
A Penny Spitfire (novella)
Talking To Owls (short stories)
Departures (short stories)
Ambiguous Encounters (short stories with Marilyn Messenger)
The Man Who Found A Barrel Full of Beer (short stories)
Other Stories & Rosie Wreay (short stories)

As Mike Smith
The Broken Mirror (poetry)
No Easy Place (poetry)
Valanga (poetry)
Martin? Extinct? (poetry)
English of the English (essays on A.E.Coppard)
Readings for Writers vol.1
The Poetic Image (a short course in the short story)
Love and Nothing Else (Readings for Writers vol.2)
The Silent Life Within (Readings for Writers vol.3)
An Early Frost (poetry)

Made in the USA
Charleston, SC
30 September 2016